Orange Juice Peas!

Lari Don
and Lizzie Wells

Ben's little sister Jessie was learning to be polite. When she said "thank you" it sounded a bit like "DA HOO".

When she said "please" it sounded exactly like "PEAS".

"Nana peas."

"Teddy peas."

"Up peas."

"Tickle peas."

On the night Mum and Dad went out to a ceilidh, Mum said to the new babysitter, "Their tea's ready, Rachel. Please give Jessie anything she wants to eat or drink because she's getting over a cold."

Mum and Dad gave Ben and Jessie a night-night cuddle, then a bye-bye wave.

Rachel gave Ben and Jessie their bowls of pasta. Then she asked, "What do you want to drink?"
Ben said, "Apple juice please."

Jessie said, "Orange juice peas."
Rachel said, "Pardon?"

"Orange juice peas."

"Really?"

Jessie nodded.

"Orange juice peas."

Rachel looked at Jessie a bit sideways. Then she went to the fridge, and found some leftover cooked peas and a carton of juice. She dropped four peas into a glass, splashed juice on top and handed it to Jessie.

Jessie said, "Da hoo," then she saw the peas floating in her juice and said,

"Yack!"

Jessie looked at Rachel and said, "Boon peas."
Rachel said, "Pardon?"

"Boon peas!" said Jessie clearly.

Rachel looked at Ben and mouthed,
"Boon?"

Ben smirked and mouthed back,

"Spoon!"

Rachel gave Jessie a spoon, with five peas balanced on it.

Jessie tipped the five
peas onto the table
and used the spoon to
fish the other peas out
of her orange juice.

She sniffed her juice, took a sip, and said,

"Yack!"

Ben giggled behind his fingers.

Jessie looked at Rachel and said, "Milk peas?"

Rachel repeated, "Milk peas?"

"No," said Jessie, "Milk PEAS!"

"Alright, if that's what you want." Rachel dropped a handful of peas into a clean glass, poured milk on top and gave it to Jessie.

Jessie said, "Da hoo," then she saw the peas bobbing in her milk.

"Yack!"

She said,
very quietly,
"Boon peas."

Rachel brought Jessie another spoon, with six peas balanced on it.

Jessie tipped the six peas onto the table and used the spoon to scoop the milky peas out of her glass.

She sniffed her milk, took a sip, and said,

"Yack!"

Ben was laughing so much he had to blow his nose.

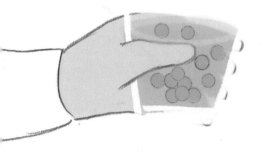

Next, Jessie asked for "Water peas." This time she could see the peas in the glass from a long way off, so she had her nose wrinkled up before the glass reached the table.

"Yack!

Boon peas!"

So Rachel brought Jessie another spoonful of peas. Jessie tipped them onto the table, and scooped the peas out of her glass as fast as she could. But the water still smelled of peas and tasted of peas.

"Yack!"

Now Ben was curled up under the table
in a ball of giggles, Jessie could hardly
see past her pile of peas, and no one had
finished their pasta.

So Rachel said, "Do you usually have pudding?"

Ben crawled out from under the table.

"Yes, we ALWAYS have pudding! Please could I have ice cream?"

Jessie wanted ice cream for pudding too.

She took a deep breath and said
very clearly,

"Ice
cream
PEAS!"

Rachel gave Jessie a bowl of ice cream with a pyramid of frozen peas on top.
  She gave Ben a bowl of ice cream with no vegetables at all.

Ben saw Jessie's eyes go all wet and shiny, and her lips wobble too much to say "Yack!"

So Ben swapped puddings. He gave his bowl of ice cream to Jessie, and he took the bowl with peas on top.

Jessie smiled and said,

"Da hoo, Ben."

Ben used his pointing finger to flick the peas off the ice cream.

Ben explained to Rachel, "Jessie says 'PEAS' when she's asking for something very politely. It doesn't mean she wants peas with everything."

"She only likes peas with fish and chips."

Ben ate up all Jessie's ice cream. Jessie ate up all Ben's ice cream. And Rachel made herself a big cup of coffee.

While Ben and Rachel searched the kitchen for escaped peas, Jessie sat down in the middle of the floor and said,

"No more peas, PEAS!"